EVERYBODY NEEDS A LITTLE

T L C

TRANSFORMATIONAL   LIFESTYLE   CONTENT

90-DAYS

of Dreams, Goals, and Intentional Living to Cultivate Passion, Purpose, and Power

PRESENTED BY

TAWAWN LOWE

www.tlc-publishing.com

Library of Congress Cataloging-in-Publication Data is available upon request.
ISBN: 979-8-9851004-1-9
E-Book ISBN: 979-8-9851004-2-6

DISCLAIMER
Although you may find the affirmative expressions helpful, the book is sold with the understanding that neither the co-authors nor TLC Publishing Company are engaged in presenting any legal, relationship, financial, emotional, or health advice. The purpose of this book is to educate and entertain. The co-authors and publishers shall neither assume liability nor responsibility for anyone concerning any loss or damage caused directly or indirectly by the information in the book.

Any person experiencing financial, anxiety, depression, health, mental health, or relationship issues should consult a licensed therapist, advisor, licensed psychologist, or another qualified professional before commencing with anything described in this book. This book is intended to provide you with the writers' insights and reflections on three subjects in the book. All results will differ; however, our goal is to provide affirmative expressions as a practical approach to fostering effective change within your life.

This book is a tribute to the person who has been my unwavering support, my mother, Charlotte Harrison. Her constant prayers, encouragement, and belief in me have been instrumental in my life's journey. Mom, I cannot thank you enough, and I love you dearly.

Furthermore, I would like to dedicate this book to all who are determined to lead a meaningful life and strive to reach their full potential. I know that your journey may not be without its challenges, but it is crucial to remember that you are not alone. We believe in you becoming the best version of yourself and creating your best life.

This book aims to uplift and motivate you, introduce new perceptions, and provide insights and guidance that will support you on your journey toward achieving your aspirations. So, together, let's embark on this journey to make your life purposeful and turn your dreams into reality.

All you need is a little TLC!

EVERYBODY NEEDS A LITTLE **TLC**

Transformational Lifestyle Content

90 Days of Intentional Living, Dreams, Goals, and Intentional Living to
Cultivate Purpose, Passion, and Power

TO: ____________________________________

FROM: _________________________________

ACKNOWLEDGMENT

THE CREATION OF the Everybody Needs a Little TLC book series is a testament to the power of collaboration and the creative minds that brought it to life. The TLC Publishing Company team deserves immense gratitude for their dedication and commitment to manifesting the vision of this book.

The collaborative co-authors are the heart and soul of this project, and their contributions cannot be overlooked. Therefore, we want to extend our most profound appreciation to each author who shared their insights, wisdom, affirming expressions, and declarations to help the life journey of individuals who need a little transformational lifestyle content (TLC).

We are incredibly grateful to these co-authors for embarking on this journey with us and for their influential writings that have the ability and the potential to motivate and empower countless individuals. Each author shared a personal part of themselves, their experiences, and the lessons they have learned through their writing, and we are honored to have their voices heard in this book.

As a collective, we are committed to leaving a footprint and legacy to impact and influence others on their journey of being, becoming, and living purposefully. We appreciate and acknowledge the contributions and support of each of these collaborative authors, who have selflessly shared their time, expertise, and wisdom to make this book a reality. Thank you for your unwavering passion and commitment to this project.

Tawawn Lowe	Simone Adams	Candice Jackson	Tia M. Norde'
Yolanda Chinn	Dr. Gail Crowder	Dr. Felicia Pratt	Stephanie Popular
Dr. Sharon Foreman	Tia Hall	Rev. Sandy Williams	

CONTENTS

ABOUT THE EVERYBODY NEEDS
A LITTLE TLC TRILOGY

THE VISIONARY OF the "Everybody Needs A Little TLC" series believes everybody needs a little TLC! Yes, we all need tender loving care, but we also need transformational lifestyle content. The type of TLC is essential to fostering change and personal growth, empowering individuals to unlock their full potential and manifest success in all facets of life.

Through her journey and as a certified transformational lifestyle coach, the Visionary behind this project is keenly aware of how our attitudes and perceptions shape our mindset, ultimately creating our reality. She recognizes the critical role mindset plays in achieving our dreams, goals, and efforts to be intentional in our living; and that our minds are a powerful tool that requires continuous care and attention, as what we put in directly impacts what we get out. The Visionary also acknowledges the tremendous power of words and how affirming language can lead to specific positive outcomes in our lives. Speaking positively about ourselves has the power to activate an inner strength that can shift our attitudes, feelings, beliefs, and intentions toward growth, happiness, self-improvement, and success. This is why she created the Everybody Needs A Little TLC trilogy and chose creative writing to present the topics shared.

The "Everybody Needs A Little TLC" trilogy is a collection of three influential books focused on nine fundamental personal development themes: self-awareness, self-esteem, self-confidence, self-worth, self-love, self-care, dream, goals, and intentional living to show their interconnectedness and the role they play in our being, becoming, and maximizing their potential. Each series presents a unique perspective and viewpoint on its designated topics allowing you to delve into your thoughts, emotions, and ideas regarding the nine personal development topics. The primary purpose of each series is to inspire change and transformation, to alter negative attitudes, adjust behaviors, and alter mentalities.

Each series employs a trifecta approach encompassing affirmative insights and wisdom, declarations, and the 90-day lifestyle change rule to achieve this goal.

The Visionary firmly believes in the potency of creative writing to empower, teach, and communicate thoughts and ideas in an engaging and thought-provoking manner. Creative writing can convey the essence of these nine personal development themes without becoming overwhelming. It presents the information in an easily understandable, relatable way and enables you to establish a meaningful connection with the themes explored in each series. The co-authors skillfully address the nine personal development themes, which possess profound significance and intricate layers of complexity. Through their distinctive tone and style, they employ literary techniques such as imagery and symbolism, enriching the exploration of these themes.

This straightforward yet compelling and efficient approach encourages self-reflection, offers alternative perspectives, and inspires transformation and change.

INTRODUCTION

WE ALL HAVE a reason for being! We were all born on purpose, with a purpose, and a big part of our life journey is to find and live our purpose. One of the ways you achieve your purpose is by cultivating your dreams, establishing your goals, and living your life with intention. However, the path to accomplishing our goals is sometimes fraught with obstacles and disappointments that make it challenging to endure. For some, envisioning their future and matching their dreams with goals may be problematic, while it may be a breeze for others. Yet, regardless of which category you are into, it is essential to recognize that these three elements - dreams, goals, and intentional living - are interdependent and necessary for helping you become the best versions of yourselves and live the most fulfilling lives possible. By consciously developing our dreams, we can identify our purpose and create a vision for our future. Then, by setting goals aligned with this vision, you can work towards achieving them in a focused way. Subsequently, living intentionally allows you to take purposeful actions that bring you closer to your daily goals.

It's essential to remember that the path towards fulfilling your purpose, becoming your best self, and achieving success is not a one-time event but rather an ongoing and dynamic process that requires you to use success habits and tools. By nurturing your dreams, setting clear goals, and living intentionally, you can bring your aspirations to fruition, unlock your full potential, and realize success. However, it's worth noting that adopting these habits and making them a lifestyle can be challenging, but the benefits are immeasurable. Cultivating these habits requires consistent effort and dedication, but they become an integral part of your lifestyle with time and practice. As you refine and sharpen these habits, you gain more clarity, purpose, and fulfillment in your life, allowing you to thrive and achieve the goals you set for yourselves.

We all should dare to dream because, within the beauty of our dreams, we can see the man or woman we want to become, how we want to show up in the world, what we want to have, and the success we want to achieve. Dreams allow you to tap into your imagination to create the life you truly desire for yourselves. But dreaming is just the start. Dreams don't come true overnight; they take time, patience, and a plan to connect your dreams with goals and bring them to reality. Your dreams need a G.P.S. that gives you the direction to reach your target.

Goals are your G.P.S. (Goal Positioning Strategy) that acts as your navigational system, guiding you from where you are now to achieving your dreams. It helps you map out the necessary steps to realize your dreams. Your G.P.S. is the instrument that keeps you focused on your goals and prompts you to take action to reach your goals. In addition, it serves as a reminder of your purpose and direction, allowing you to remain on course despite setbacks. By developing a clear G.P.S., you can overcome any roadblocks that stand in your way and move towards your dreams with intention and purpose.

To make the most of your G.P.S., it is crucial to be intentional about your dreams and the journey toward reaching your destination. Your G.P.S. provides a roadmap toward achieving your goals, but it is up to you to stay focused on your dreams and take consistent action. Being intentional means being mindful of your efforts and making decisions that align with your vision, passions, and values. It means staying committed to yourself, your dreams, goals and being willing to make the necessary sacrifices to achieve them. By using your G.P.S. with intention, you live intentionally and purposefully.

Dreams, goals, and intentional living are not just vague concepts; they are essential principles for personal and professional success that can help you discover your purpose, find your passion, and unlock your full potential. In this book, we aim to provide you with creative insights and wisdom that will help you understand the interdependence of these success principles and the importance of having them in your success toolkit. Throughout 90 days, the creative affirmative insights, wisdom, and declarations, we will consistently challenge you to evaluate your beliefs and thoughts, identify your barriers, take action, and assess how you can hone these success principles and integrate them to achieve success in all aspects of your life.

Overview of the Book

Everybody Needs A Little TLC 90 Days of Dreams, Goals, and Intentional Living to Cultivate Purpose, Passion, and Power Body" contains creative works that skillfully weave together three fundamental aspects of personal development: dreams, goals, and intentional living. Like the other two series within the Everybody Needs A Little TLC trilogy, this book is structured with a trifecta approach that explores the three themes in three discrete sections. This trifecta approach includes affirmative expressions and insights, declarations, and the 90 concept to develop a lifestyle change to help you embark on a transformative journey. Affirmative expressions, insights, and wisdom are artfully communicated to encourage you to look inward, and offer diverse perspectives for your consideration, present ideas, and strategies. The declarations will instill positive self-talk and emphasize the importance of affirming and speaking positivity into your life. The 90-day concept is designed to help you develop a consistent pattern that creates new habits and lifestyle changes around the three success habits and add dreams, goals, and intentional living to your success toolkit.

The authors provide the readers with various helpful insights, words of wisdom, affirmations, and declarations aimed at promoting a shift in mentality to assist with believing in yourself, empowering yourself, becoming your greatest self, and creating your best life. Who we are, whom we become, what we create, and what we choose to accomplish in life are all heavily influenced by how we see the world and the beliefs we harbor within ourselves.

Within the pages of this book, we aim to remind you of the importance of dreams, goals, and intentional living and encourage you to focus on sharpening those areas of your life, so you can be empowered to be, become, and live your best life.

How to use this Book?

There are various ways to incorporate the TLC trilogy it into your daily routine:

1. For 90 days, start and end your day by reading the daily insight/affirmative expression and reciting the declaration three times.
2. Reflect on what resonated with you, journal your thoughts and feelings, and what the words mean.
3. Randomly select a day and use the mirror talk technique to recite the daily insight and declaration before a mirror.
4. Discuss the daily insight with friends, read the declaration together, and journal your takeaways.
5. Record the insight and declaration and listen to it throughout the day.

Remember, there is no right or wrong way to use this book. However, it is essential to dedicate time to the process, incorporate it into your daily routine, and make affirmations a part of your success habits. Stay present, use mindfulness when reading the insights and declarations, and visualize yourself in each of the 90-day expressions.

The Journey Begins!

We are grateful you chose to prioritize self-investment by reading this book. We believe that as you study the material, your life will improve. Through the Everybody Needs a Little TLC Series, we at TLC-Publishing Company want to inspire and equip our readers. We hope that by thinking about the guidance, insights, wisdom, and affirmations offered in this book, you will be inspired and fully grasp the relevance of your dreams, goals, and intentional living in establishing the foundation for your success.

"90 Days of Dreams, Goals, and Intentional Living to Cultivate Purpose, Passion, Power, and Success» is a book that will resonate strongly with individuals who value employing proven success techniques and personal development concepts to improve and create their best lives. The book will also be a powerful reminder to those who dare to dream, set goals, and live consciously to stay the course and incorporate these ideas into their success arsenal.

This book is for those who are hesitant about dreaming or dreaming BIG, possibly due to a fear of failure or the unknown. Without a distinct path to follow, such individuals may struggle to identify their true desires and aspirations and may lack direction in life. Significant accomplishments can be difficult for them, leaving them feeling trapped and unable to escape their current situation. They may also lack knowledge of how to create a meaningful existence with intention.

In addition, it is a fantastic resource for people needing a simple yet effective approach to contribute towards their overall personal and professional development. Finally, it serves as a reminder that everyone needs a little TLC on their path to a better version of themselves and achieving success. This book can revolutionize your life by emphasizing the importance of who you become and what you do. You can alter your attitude, viewpoint, and trajectory within 90 days. The question is, are you prepared for this change? Dreams, goals, and intentional living are achievable with devotion and attention.

It's time...time to give yourself a little TLC!

Tawawn Lowe

DREAMS

A mental way to explore the possibilities...
Seeds in pictures, images, and ideas form in your subconscious mind as messages that awaken possibilities within your heart and soul, evoking action that pushes you toward your purpose, passion, and potential.

Beloved,

The gift of dreaming is one of the powerful blessings that God has bestowed upon you. Your imagination is a valuable tool that can help you envision every aspect of your life. As a dreamer, it is crucial to nurture this gift and not let anything obstruct your innate ability to dream, imagine, and create a vision for your future.

By cultivating a state of creative flow and tapping into your imagination and dreams, you can unlock the profound connection between them and the ability to craft a vision for your life. So don't be afraid to dream big and allow the purity of a childlike imagination to reignite your creativity and inspire you to envision your life's path.

Remember that you are never too old to dream a new dream or revisit your childhood aspirations. Your dreams are the keys that unlock the doors to your happiness, love, success, prosperity, and peace. Without them, life loses its excitement, and you miss the endless possibilities it can bring.

So, permit yourself to dream limitlessly, let your dreams motivate and inspire you, and challenge you to step outside your comfort zone. Embrace your identity as a dreamer and take your dreams seriously because they are vital to manifesting your life vision, nurturing your creativity, and propelling you to the next level of success.

Remember that great things begin in your imagination, and seeing is believing. God has blessed you with the ability to dream, so dare to dream and cultivate your dream esteem. Let your dreams become the stepping stones to creating a vision for your future and manifesting your desired life.

Dreams are Like Seeds!

DREAMS ARE LIKE seeds; they hold the potential for growth and transformation. Just as a seed needs to be nurtured and tended to, our dreams require effort and commitment to come to fruition. With time, care, and determination, our dreams can bloom into something beautiful and full of life.

Dreams provide us with direction and purpose, helping us to focus our efforts and channel our energy towards meaningful goals. They give us hope and inspiration, fueling our motivation and keeping us moving forward, even in adversity.

Dreams, like seeds, can be fragile and easily damaged. They are vulnerable to the crushing effects of negative thinking, self-doubt, and lack of confidence. So, it's crucial to guard our hopes and aspirations, foster a growth attitude, and have faith in our skills.

Our dreams are a powerful force for change, and like seeds, they can shape our lives and bring about positive transformation. So, let us hold on to our dreams, tend to them with care, and watch as they bloom into something beautiful and full of life.

<u>DECLARATION</u>: Today, I will let my dreams take root as the seeds of my future life.

Tawawn Lowe

Child Like Dreams!

LETTING YOUR IMAGINATION run wild, like a child, is a liberating and rejuvenating experience.

Allow yourself to escape the constraints of reality and enter a world where anything is possible. Permit your childlike sense of wonder and boundless creativity to bring a new perspective, fresh ideas, and a renewed sense of excitement to your life. Let it be a reminder that the imagination is a powerful tool that can bring joy and inspiration into your life, regardless of age. So let your imagination soar, let it be free, and enjoy the thrill of the unknown, just like a child.

It's time to reawaken our sense of wonder and dream again.

DECLARATION: I declare my determination to rekindle my creativity, break free from restraints, and allow myself to dream of the destiny I genuinely wish for.

Tawawn Lowe

Day 3

Dreams are Meant to Come True

MANY OF US are afraid our dreams will not come true. That fear is realized if you don't pursue your heart's desires. Your dreams are creative ideas for you to nourish and launch out into the deep. It's unknown whether you will succeed or fail. What is most important is that you shake off fear and doubt and try it. Don't just sit idly by, and don't hold back because the effort is all up to you. Strive and go after your creative ideas and dreams. Pursue your vision and see what happens. A dream realized is like discovering a whole new world. The world you imagined and thought about day after day. The journey to get there is paved with success, setbacks, joy, and tears of disappointment. But when the dream comes alive, it will be more significant and impactful than ever imagined. Dreams are meant to come true!

<u>DECLARATION</u>: Today, I will follow my dream(s).

Rev. Sandy Williams

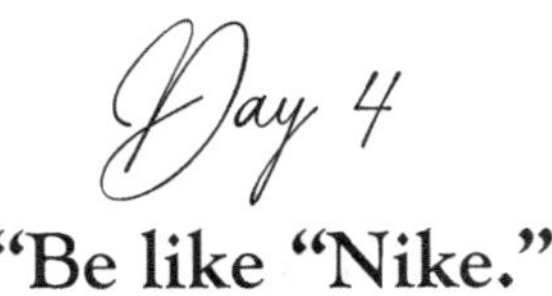

"Be like "Nike."

LIFE, INDEED, IS what you make it. Evaluate yours to determine if you are living the life you want or if there is a need for adjustments. If you are unhappy, it is up to you to make the necessary changes to obtain the happiness you desire.

You can measure how far off you are from your desired lifestyle and identify some steps you need to take to get there. Anything is possible, within reason, if you set realistic goals to achieve it.

Write your action plan, and make it plain, precise, and visible daily. Be fearless in your approach to the tasks. You have lollygagged long enough in your current situation, so you desire something new. Stop hemming and hawing over what's been, what's not, and what could be! Instead, press the reset button to activate your new action plan toward a life that will generate newfound joy, peace, comfort, confidence, and success you always knew you could attain.

This life is too short to waste any more time falling prey to naysayers or conforming to what family, friends, or society says is best for you. You know what's better for you than anyone else, so stop BS'ing! Be like "Nike" and just do it.

<u>DECLARATION</u>: Today, I will evaluate my current circumstances, make necessary adjustments, and move forward, fearlessly approaching life according to my desired plan of attainable success for my peace of mind and happiness.

Tia Norde'

Day 5

Build Your Dream Esteem!

D – Driven and determined to reach your destiny.

R – Resilient, resourceful, and rising to your fullest potential.

E – Empowered and equipped to evolve to the next level of your life.

A – Activating into action to achieve your Goals.

M – Making moves to manifest your DREAMS into reality.

S – Strengthening your self-esteem and self-confidence.

<u>DECLARATION</u>: Today, I will build my dream esteem muscle and dare to dream the impossible for my life.

Tawawn Lowe

It's Never Too Late!

IT IS NEVER too late to make a change, to do what your heart desires, and to live the life you've always dreamed of living. Because age is simply a number, you shouldn't let your age prevent you from following your goals and ambitions.

No matter where you are in life or what stage you are in, it is your responsibility to pursue and make your dreams and goals a reality. Embrace each new phase of your life as an opportunity to continue maturing, gaining knowledge, and following your interests. Never use your age as an excuse for not going after the life you want to live because your potential and possibilities are essentially endless.

<u>DECLARATION</u>: Today, I will adjust my attitude from believing I'm too old to pursue my dreams – to believing it's never too late.

Tawawn Lowe

Dreams Versus Fears

CLOSE YOUR EYES. Take a deep breath. Now Dream. Create a picture of a vacation you want to take, the outfit you can't wait to wear, and the date (with your "person" or friends). Can you see yourself there? Now, what would stop you from making that dream a reality?

When you opened your eyes, did you think about your financial situation? Your weight? Your schedule? Did you start to tell yourself all the reasons why those will be dreams? STOP! Don't let those fears keep those dreams in your head. Instead, allow those dreams to be greater than your fears. Allow your wants for those dreams to outweigh whoever or whatever says you can't have them. Allow your actions to speak louder for your dreams than your stumbling blocks.

You can manifest your dreams. You will manifest your dreams. You will allow your dreams to be greater than your fears.

DECLARATION: Today, I will push past my fears to manifest my dreams because my dreams are more significant than my fears.

Candice Jackson

Give Your Dreams Wings

ASK YOURSELF, "WHAT are those aspirations in life that I dared to dream out loud?" When you speak to them aloud, do you feel nervous, foolish, or fearful?

Where is that feeling in your body? Butterflies in your belly? Tension in your jaw?

Knowing where this uneasiness resides in your body is essential because it behooves you not to be distracted when you take flight.

So, learn and know yourself. Acknowledge YES; you want this, and it makes you feel this way. Allow those physical reminders, be it a queasy stomach or clenched teeth, to serve as a gauge on your flight control panel. Remember, it's not a surprise if you are monitoring it.

Craft your wings with the passion that fuels your dreams.

Unfurl them, flap, and admiringly take in the entire expansion that is you.

Know that your expansion is for you and takes nothing from anyone else.

Daily Visualize what it means to soar and Drink in the Beauty of that Flight.

May that Experience be the reinforcement tape that plays in your mind, that fills your heart and nourishes your soul.

DECLARATION: Today, I will unfurl wings and unapologetically take up space so my dreams may soar. I acknowledge those hesitant parts, yet I trust my wings to carry me to the next level of my journey.

Tia Hall

Day 9

It's Just Your Imagination

IMAGINATION IS A formidable force within your mind, granting you the ability to visualize and create mental images that can transport you to new realms of possibility. It opens the door and paves the way to creativity, recognizing potential, and creating a vivid picture of your desires for change, happiness, healing, peace, and success.

It is the fuel that drives your dreams and aspirations, enabling you to be creative, to see hope in adversity, and to bring your wildest ideas to life.

Harness the power of your imagination and let it shape your vision for a brighter future, for it truly is a superpower waiting to be unleashed."

DECLARATION: Today and every day, I will tap into my superpower to manifest a vision for every area of my life.

Tawawn Lowe

Dreams are Necessary!

WITHOUT DREAMS, THERE will be no ambition to chase. There will be no goals to reach. The world would be void of creativity and progression.

Life would be black and white, lacking the color needed to make it beautiful. We would all be empty without dreams.

Not having dreams is like following an invisible shadow. It's a wild goose chase. We must give ourselves permission to dream and pursue those ambitions.

We can't achieve color in our life or this world without goals, and we need to dream for these goals.

<u>DECLARATION</u>: Today, I CHOOSE to add color to my life and this world by living out my dreams.

Tawawn Lowe

Don't Wake Me – I'm Dreaming

I SAID IT once before, so I'll say it again, "Stop laughing at your dreams!" It's time to get them out of your head and make them a reality. I'm a firm believer that dreams aren't just made for sleeping. Think about it, it started as a mere thought...became a dream, and now it can be a reality.

What gives you butterflies (good ones)? What excites you? Remember to dream. Your best you is waiting inside of you. I challenge you every day to go from daydreaming to living your dreams. However, you do it, whatever it is. Your dreams are worth shooting your shot. Trust yourself, your abilities, and your unique talents to emote a reality that only you can birth. The world is waiting for your possibilities to become a reality.

I'm sure you can recall waking up from a dream that you did not want to end. Perhaps you even tried falling asleep, hoping to revisit that dream. It was so good and seemed so real. Only to find it wasn't real, but just a dream. As good as it was, it wasn't real. No matter how real it seemed. Well, I'm here to tell you that when you start living your dreams, and I'm speaking from where your dreams become a reality, initially, if you feel like it's a dream, you'll want to pinch yourself because you can hardly believe it. Then you quickly realize you're awake, and yes, this is, in fact, a dream that has become a reality.

Yes, your vision can become your reality. Your dreams can come true too. The only thing that's stopping it is YOU!

Again, the bottom line is that they're- Your Dreams. It's time to live them.

<u>DECLARATION</u>: Today, I will Dream Big and live out my dreams.

Yolanda "Loni" Chinn

Dreams Are POSSIBLE!

YOUR BIG-PICTURE GOALS can keep you going. They provide motivation and fuel for life. Unfortunately, many settle for less than the best life they can live, but you can decide today that you'll accept no less than the fulfillment of your dreams.

The key is to keep putting one foot in front of the other, taking small steps toward your dreams. But, at the same time, continually visualize what your life looks like at the finish line.

Steps To Make Your Dreams Come True:
1. To realize your dreams, you must take massive, consistent action daily.
2. Turn a small dream into a large one by thinking big.
3. Staying brave when challenges come.
4. Surround yourself with encouraging and helpful people with dreams bigger than yours.
5. Remember, your dreams are an extension and expression of your identity.

<u>DECLARATION</u>: Today, the only thing stopping ME from achieving my most important dreams is ME!

Dr. Gail Crowder

It's Okay if Your Dreams Scare You

YOUR DREAMS ARE always outside of your comfort zone. Pursuing your dreams requires conscious effort, growth, and change; this can feel somewhat uncomfortable initially. You may experience some fears and worries, but this is normal. You don't need to focus on the fears but on the dreams. This way, your dreams become more important to you than your fears.

<u>DECLARATION</u>: Today, I CHOOSE, push past my fears, and step outside my comfort zone to pursue my dreams.

Tawawn Lowe

The Dream vs. The Reality of the Dream

WE ALL HAVE a dream. There is something in each of us that we want to achieve. Everyone's dream is different and on a different scale, but it's still a dream. We work, and we work. We hit goals and goals and reached all our milestones, and still, we are chasing the dream. Sometimes it may feel like that dream is unattainable, and we will NEVER get it. But did you know that you could be living your dream at this very moment?

The dream looks fabulous, unique, and glamorous, but your life now feels nothing like the dream you imagined. That's because what you didn't see in the dream was the hard work, long days, and moments of struggle. Your dream was what the world sees, not what you, the actual person living the dream, are going through.

Don't discount the small milestones that show you are living that dream.

<u>DECLARATION</u>: Today, I CHOOSE and acknowledge that at this very moment, I am leaving my dream.

Dr. Felicia Pratt

The Gift of Trusting!

MAKING A GOAL and writing it down is the first step to achieving a dream. But a dream is just an image in your head until you speak it forth into existence. The power of the tongue inspires life. So, proclaim your dream in the way you talk and the way you walk intentionally.

Making a goal and stepping out in faith is the second step to achieving a dream. Fasten your dream to hope for new realities. The power of the tongue inspires life. Proclaim your dream in the way you live it, intentionally.

Making a goal and stepping out with trust is the third step to achieving a dream. Put the dream in the space of hope, knowing and believing in new possibilities. The power of the tongue inspires life. Proclaim your dream in the way you sustain it, intentionally.

<u>DECLARATION</u>: Today, I CHOOSE to embrace the power of the tongue to speak forth my dreams with faith as the cornerstone, sustained by the gift of hope, trusting intentionally.

Dr. Sharon Foreman

Day 16

Be A BIG DREAMER!

IF YOU ARE going to dream, you might as well dream BIG! It will cost you nothing but activating your imagination into a journey of unlimited possibilities. So, close your eyes, take the limits off, and allow your imagination to lead you on a journey that brings forth your future.

<u>**DECLARATION**</u>: Today, I CHOOSE to Dream Big and let those dreams lead me to my future.

Tawawn Lowe

The Beauty of Your Dreams!

YOUR DREAMS ARE beautiful because they will direct you and help you discover your inner talents, who you want to be, and what you are made of.

The beauty of your dreams will give you creative insight to solve those big or little life issues you would never have predicted.

The beauty of your dreams will motivate you to keep trying because your vision for your life is bigger than your circumstances.

The beauty of your dreams will allow you to see beyond your natural eyes and operate in FAITH to what you want to manifest.

The beauty of your dreams will inspire you to take a bold step forward and see the world as the stage from which you create yourself and build your legacy.

<u>DECLARATION</u>: Today, I CHOOSE to see the beauty of my dreams and take bold steps to manifest the vision.

Stephanie Poplar

Day 18

Imagine Another Reality!

IF YOUR LIFE doesn't look like you want it, take creative license in your brain, let your imagination wander, and start imagining yourself and your future in the reality you want for yourself. Let your dreams be big, bold, scary, and exciting.

<u>**DECLARATION**</u>: Today, I CHOOSE to take creative license in my brain and let my imagination give me a new vision for my life.

Simone Adams

Seeing is Believing!

BELIEVE IN THE power of your vision. Seeing opens your eyes, mind, and heart to endless possibilities. Embrace the beauty and potential of what you see and have faith that what you believe in can become a reality. Believing is not just about having faith; it's about trusting in yourself and the power of your perceptions. Combining the two unlocks a world of potential where anything becomes possible, and dreams come to life. Remember, seeing is not just a passive act but an active one that has the power to shape your destiny.

So, believe in what you see, and see the beauty in what you believe.

<u>DECLARATION</u>: Today, I will proclaim my faith by believing in and taking action toward my dreams.

Tawawn Lowe

<h1 style="text-align:center;">Day 20</h1>

Make Your Dream a Reality for the World!

YOUR DREAM IS a valuable part of you. Your dream is a part of who you are and why you exist. Your dream is the answer to someone else's prayer or problem. Dreams are a part of manifesting change in the world! You are that change agent. Your dream is waiting to be manifested into reality. Visualize and walk out the vision. Make a plan and take action. Birthing pains, growth challenges, and tears of joy are part of bringing your dream into reality. The dream is already conceived in your mind; now nourish it with your actions and fertilize it with the help of others. The world is waiting for your dream to manifest.

<u>**DECLARATION**</u>: Today, I will take action to manifest my dream.

Rev. Sandy Williams

Is It a Dream, or A Dream Deferred?

DON'T LET YOUR dreams be deferred; pursue them passionately and passionately. Your dreams are part of who you are and deserve to be realized. So, no matter what obstacles may come your way, never give up on what you truly desire and what brings meaning to your life.

It's important to remember that the journey toward your dreams may not always be easy, but it is worth it. Surround yourself with people who support and encourage you, and keep your focus on your goals, no matter how difficult the road may seem.

Take small, consistent steps toward your dreams, and celebrate every little victory. Remember that progress, no matter how small, is still progress. But most importantly, believe in yourself and your abilities to make your dreams a reality.

Don't let your dreams be deferred; keep them alive by never giving up on what you truly desire and what brings meaning to your life.

<u>**DECLARATION**</u>: Today and every day, I CHOOSE to take steps to keep my dreams alive.

Tawawn Lowe

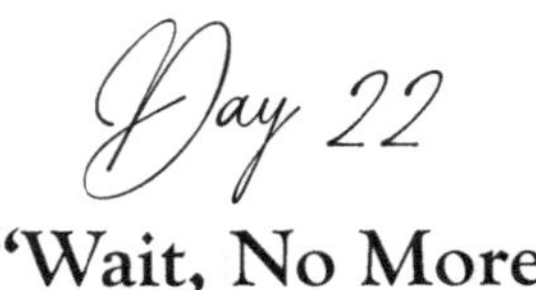

Day 22

"Wait, No More"

BELIEVE IN YOURSELF more than you expect others to believe in you, and don't let anyone or anything interfere with that vision. Believing in what you are capable of, and knowing who you are capable of being, are two different things. Belief in yourself dictates your behavior, and understanding yourself impacts your perception and drive. Being in tune with both determines what actions are applied in decision-making toward life circumstances and opportunities.

Success is what you want it to be, so identify what that is for you. Trust in your abilities, commit to the work to attain the goal, and proudly partake in the fruits of your labor because you've earned it. Don't be consumed by your or anyone else's fear; allow it to motivate you. We all do what we want, when we want, as capable of doing it. So, figure out what you want to do, be or achieve, and don't stop striving to achieve it until your dream has become your reality. The only thing slowing down your progress is your thought process. Take time now to build the life of your dreams so that you can live, having the time of your life before your time runs out.

<u>**DECLARATION:**</u> To wait is to die a slow death, so today, I CHOOSE to live with zero regrets, and I recognize that anyone who has something to say about it doesn't want to die alone.

Tia Norde'

Day 23

This is Your Permission to DREAM BIG!

DREAMING BIG IS not only about setting big goals. It's also about embracing a mindset of possibility and tapping into the power of your imagination to create a brighter future. When you dream big, you send a powerful message to your subconscious that you can achieve great things.

So, go ahead, dare to dream big, and don't be afraid to imagine the unimaginable.

This is your permission to dream big. Embrace the power of your imagination, set your sights high, and believe anything is possible. The world is your canvas, and it's time to unleash the power of your dreams.

<u>DECLARATION</u>: Today, I affirm that I am permitting myself to dream big and believe in the limitless possibilities of my future.

Tawawn Lowe

Day 24
Déjà vu!

WEBSTER'S DICTIONARY DEFINES Deja vu as "a feeling of having already experienced the present situation." But in French, it means "already seen." Isn't that what a dream is? Something you've already seen in your mind.

I've had déjà vu moments. I know you have as well. But what if they are already something we've dreamed of and don't remember? What else have I dreamed that I have manifested? So, imagine what you enjoy now because you dared to dream about it.

Tomorrow when you wake up, ask your dreams to reveal themselves to you. Ask them to manifest what it needs, whether it's a precaution to move away from something or an encouragement to move toward something. Then, the next time you have a déjà vu moment, be thankful you are a dreamer.

<u>**DECLARATION**</u>: Today, I ask you to remember my dreams and recognize what they are telling me.

Candice Jackson

The Dream is Free, but the Hustle is Real!

THE BEAUTY OF having a dream is that it's free, a gift from the universe to be cherished and nurtured. Your dreams are not just fleeting thoughts but are alive with purpose and potential.

The hustle is where the rubber meets the road. The hustle is where the grind begins. Where the long hours take place, the sacrifices take place, and the pouring of your blood, sweat, and tears. The hustle separates the dreamers from the doers, and success awaits those willing to work for it.

The dream may be free, but the hustle is real, and it requires us to show up every day and put in the effort to make our dreams a reality.

The reward of turning your dreams into a reality is beyond measure, so don't be afraid to hustle and grind.

Remember, the dream is free, but the hustle is real.

<u>**DECLARATION**</u>: Today, I acknowledge that success in achieving my dreams requires hard work and dedication, and I am willing to pay the price.

Tawawn Lowe

Wake Up!

WHEN WE IGNORE our dreams, we fall into a deep sleep. Dreams are meant to be awakened. Dreams develop in the safe place of our hearts and minds. Dreams are meant to inspire and guide us into action. Dreams are our creative aspirations waiting to be executed. Dreams manifest through the spiritual awakening of our thoughts. Wake up and put your dreams into action. Wake up and act on your hopes and desires. Wake up and dream out loud. Wake up and let others see you are present and no longer sleeping. Wake up and activate your creative thoughts. Wake up and present your ideas to the world. Wake up and do what you were created to do. Wake up and live out your dream. A dream activated and fulfilled is a life well lived. So don't continue to slumber; wake up and live your life!

<u>DECLARATION</u>: Today, I will wake up and live out my dream.

Rev. Sandy Williams

Dreams Stretch Your Imagination

A RUSH OF excitement awaits when you plunge into the depths of your imagination.

Dive in, indulge your curiosities, and let your inner child out to play. Feel the sheer joy of your past and present and channel that energy. Put your logical mind on pause and give way to your feelings. Take charge of your imagination and the world of possibility. After all, dreaming is simply an invitation to explore the never-ending trails of possibilities.

<u>**DECLARATION**</u>: Today, I will seize the opportunity to expand the depth of my imagination.

Tawawn Lowe

Dreams are Worth Chasing!

DREAMS ARE WORTH chasing. Your dreams are worth chasing. When you pursue your dreams, you'll find that your life has meaning and purpose. So run, run fast, and chase the possibilities that sit within your dreams. and

The dreams you dream are not just about you. They can alter people's lives and positively impact the world if you take calculated risks and go past your comfort zone.

Your dreams aren't just about you; they have the power to impact and inspire other people in ways that you might not have ever imagined were even possible.

The world is waiting for your dreams to be manifested.

<u>DECLARATION</u>: Today, I will chase my dreams not just for me but for the others they might impact.

Simone Adams

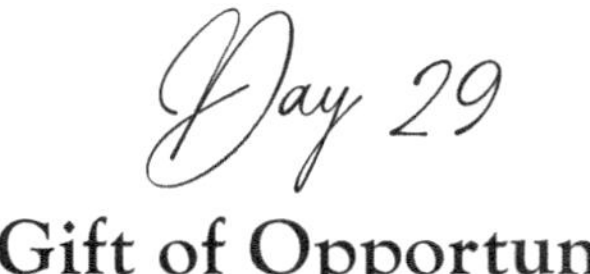

Gift of Opportunity

LIFE IS A gift of opportunity to live in abundance. It would be best if you always strive to reach your maximum potential. Every day you awake is another gift of opportunity to implement a plan, strategy, or technique to achieve goals you've imagined for yourself, towards a life of joy, freedom, peace of mind, and accomplishment you've always desired. You can do anything you want in life with proper execution, timing, and applied effort consistently. Sacrifice, discipline, good work ethic, and follow-through will aid the process. Patience, faith, belief in self, and your ability to persist through obstacles will propel you along the way when the journey becomes long, challenging, and seemingly impossible. No matter what, stay the course and never give up on yourself or your dream. You may not get there when you thought you would, but if you keep striving, you'll get there right on time when it's most worth wild. You will look back, admire the journey, and embrace it ALL, good, bad, and indifferent. Anything worth having is worth the sacrifice and effort, especially when maximizing the potential to be your best version of yourself.

<u>**DECLARATION**</u>: Today, I CHOOSE to no longer settle for just existing. I will live with intention, striving to be the best me and not waste another day of opportunity!

Tia Norde'

It's Time to Rumble!

DREAMS ARE THE factors in our life that encourage us to live, make every day an adventure, and cause us to reach for the stars. But unfortunately, so many people have trouble seeing the potential of their dreams. So, they give up on them because they don't know how they will come true. But you and your dreams are worth fighting for, so you gotta put up your dukes and start punching.

Fighting for your dreams means pursuing them with determination and resilience, despite obstacles and setbacks. It entails being willing to take risks, strong enough to overcome obstacles, and dedicated enough to keep trying when things become difficult. So put on your gloves, step into that ring, square up with your goals and dreams, and start punching until you knock every one of them out - and they are done. Don't be scared to bob and weave; lean on the ropes if you get a little tired; when you get knocked out, catch your wind, and jump back. Fight for your dreams to prove your worth and your convictions to yourself.

Fighting for your dreams—whether for yourself or the benefit of others—is what gives your life meaning and purpose. In other words, no matter how difficult things get, you should never stop fighting for your desired future. If you are willing to fight, you can make your dreams a reality. So, are you ready to rumble?

DECLARATION: Today, I CHOOSE, step into the ring of life, and fight courageously and passionately to manifest my dreams.

Tawawn Lowe

GOALS

The cornerstone upon which you lay the foundation of your life's masterpiece. Goals provide the blueprints and structure necessary to bring your life vision to reality, brick by brick. Whether short-term or long-term, each goal is a building block that brings you closer to realizing your full potential and creating a life filled with meaning, purpose, and accomplishments.

Beloved,

You are not merely meant to be a dreamer but a goal-seeker. You can transform your dreams into a tangible reality with the divine gifts bestowed upon you. Moreover, you have been blessed with the strength, talent, and drive to pursue your goals passionately.

Goals are the breaths that give life to your dreams and give them the air they need to take flight and soar. They offer a framework for the actions you need to take to turn your dreams into a reality. When you set clear and achievable goals, you give yourself a roadmap for achieving your life vision. Your goals are the fuel that drives you toward fulfilling your dreams. They keep you focused and motivated, even in the face of challenges and obstacles. And when you work towards your goals with faith and determination, you open a world of endless possibilities and opportunities.

So, rise and take hold of your purpose. Let your unwavering determination guide you on a journey toward a purpose-driven life. Trust in God's plan for you and know your goals are within reach, waiting for you to claim them. Every step you take toward your goals will draw you closer to the breathtaking beauty and power of your dreams becoming a reality.

Remember, God has gifted you with everything you need to achieve greatness. Harness the divine gifts within you and use them to create a life of purpose and passion. So go forth, set your goals, and watch as your dreams take flight and soar.

EVERYBODY NEEDS A LITTLE TLC

Legacy Building Blocks

CREATING A LEGACY is my ultimate dream, starting with setting audacious goals. I envision a future where my accomplishments, passion, and hard work live on, inspiring future generations.

My goals serve as the building blocks of this legacy, each representing a step towards a greater purpose. I pour my heart and soul into each goal, knowing that the impact I make today will ripple into the future.

By striving for excellence and leaving a lasting impact, I am planting the seeds of a legacy that will continue to flourish long after I am gone.

<u>DECLARATION</u>: Today, I AFFIRM that my dreams and goals are crucial for my success and building blocks for a legacy I will leave for the next generation.

Tawawn Lowe

Give It Your All

GAZE INTO THE dark of the night. Then, look above and see the stars shining brightly.

Imagine reaching beyond the moon-lite sky. Follow the dreams of your mind's eye.

Take one step at a time. If you stumble, if you waiver, or if you fall.

Get back up and continue to give it you're all.

Focus your thoughts and make it your intent to obtain your goal by recovering from every failure or bad event.

Look and imagine all the endless possibilities.

Leap forward on faith and pray on bended knees.

It's all about taking risks and not playing it safe.

Everyone knows it takes a lot of effort to win a race.

Pressing forward may also include falling back.

However, you must never give up or give in to lack.

Keep moving forward and give it your all.

<u>DECLARATION</u>: Today, I CHOOSE, not give in to setbacks or stumbling blocks.

Rev. Sandy Williams

"When...NOW is a WIN!"

WHEN AN OPPORTUNITY presents itself, please don't wait for it to disappear before taking advantage of it. Don't make excuses for missing out on it, trying to justify your lackadaisical approach. Procrastination is not a trait of winners. Winners are Go-getters, always ready for their next opportunity to win.

When you don't plan, you fail, which is unacceptable to winners. It's not to say that winners don't fail, but winners don't quit until they win. Making constant adjustments to your plan until it becomes a winning strategy plan is acceptable and recommended. A plan provides structure to the foundation on which you want to build your dreams and goals. Without a blueprint, you can't build; without structure, there's no stability, and without order to maintain focus and motivation towards reaching your goal, there isn't one.

Don't allow mediocrity to interfere with achieving your greatest potential. You are above average and created with the intent for purpose! You are capable of everything you think of, qualified, and equipped to do the job. A little can go a long way, but nothing will get you nowhere. People do what they want when they want, so where does that leave you?

<u>DECLARATION</u>: Today, I DECLARE; this is my time to step up and get in the game! I can't let another opportunity pass me by if I want to be who I desire to be! I will never say never because never is not an option for a winner unless it's NEVER QUIT!

I CAN AND WILL WIN!

Tia Norde'

Fitting the Pieces Together

GOALS ARE THE missing pieces to the puzzle of your life, waiting to be found and fit into place to reveal the complete picture of your dreams and aspirations. Each goal you set, each step you take towards its realization, brings you closer to completing the picture and discovering the beauty within.

Whether personal or professional, big or small, your goals connect every aspect of your life, forming a tapestry of growth, progress, and accomplishments. So, gather your goals, align them with your dreams, purpose, and talents, and start piecing together the puzzle of your life. When each goal is achieved, it clicks into place, adding another layer of richness and depth to the tapestry of your life.

So, embrace the challenge of discovering where the pieces go, the excitement of connecting each piece, watch as your goals become a work of art, and bask in the beauty of a life lived to its fullest potential.

<u>DECLARATION</u>: Today, I CHOOSE to embrace the journey of connecting the pieces of my life puzzle, piece by piece, to reveal the masterpieces from my dreams.

Tawawn Lowe

Archery and Goals

GET YOUR MIND, Body Bows, and Arrows ready. Goals in life are your targets.

What are you doing with your mind, body, and resources to hit your targets?

An archer must physically prepare to embody the stamina and strength needed for this endeavor. One must practice focusing and quieting their mind to see and accurately aim clearly. Archers also become one with their bow.

Be ready to devote yourself to your goals.

Ascertain what disciplines you must practice to build your strength and stamina. Take time regularly to quiet your mind and focus on your goals. Be mindful that outside conditions can shift your target, hold the presence of mind to change and move accordingly.

Remember, the goal is the target, but the craft and development of oneself is the TRUE AIM. So now up your game and GO.

DECLARATION: Today, I CHOOSE to devote myself to my goals by building my strength and stamina for the work. I will quiet my mind to keep my focus sharp and accurate. And I know the development of myself is the truest of aims.

Tia Hall

Doing Well, By Doing Good!

WE'RE ALWAYS PREPARING for something greater. Dream Big...Set Goals... Take Action. That's the usual script for goal setting. The best way to get ahead is to get started. If you become tired and weary, learn to rest and not quit. Choosing the path for your life is your choice. While it can be difficult sometimes to accomplish, once you decide, the next step is an action plan. Your plan of action will always require you to do something. You will likely need to research, study, plan, network, and yes- Do. So, let's get to it.

Create the life you want to live. What are you waiting for? Be strategic about your actions with everything, from finance to romance, and make sure you are making smart moves and are well with your decisions. The bumps in the road will be there. Don't be discouraged by them; I like to think of them as speedbumps instead of roadblocks. Sometimes those bumps in the road are enough to slow you down but not stop you- so don't let them.

You know, you can provide or offer value to a person. What can you offer? You can also assist someone with a goal or two within your busy schedule. Successful people typically are interested in helping people. Connections you have with others, your core connections usually place you with resources and passions like yours, so don't be reluctant to assist as long as it does not get in the way of your goals. Remember, all goals are not created equally.

You can make it! You can do it!

<u>DECLARATION</u>: Today, I CHOOSE to set out to achieve my goals. I will do what it takes.

Yolanda "Loni" Chinn

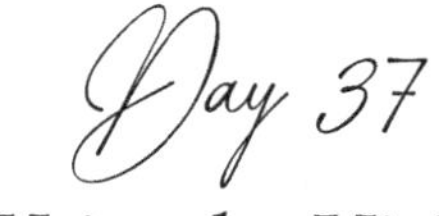

Write the Vision!

GOALS, LIKE DREAMS, need to be put down in writing. The power of manifestation lies in putting pen and paper into your dreams and aspirations. When you write down your goals, you bring them to life and make them tangible and real.

The written word is a powerful tool for visualization, and it can help you stay motivated and focused as you work toward your aspirations. By writing down your goals, you give yourselves a roadmap and a clear vision of what you want to achieve. It is said that 'what you see, you will be drawn to which is undoubtedly true regarding your goals.

So, write down your goals and watch as they become a reality before your very eyes."

<u>DECLARATION</u>: Today, I AFFIRM my dreams and aspirations to life by putting them in writing.

Tawawn Lowe

Day 38

Turning The Invisible into The Visible

THE ISSUE IS that traditional goal-setting techniques often don't work for most women. This is a tragic setup that typically results in situations where even if you are working toward a goal, you feel defeated and less content than when you started.

Before setting a worthwhile goal, you must connect with the truth of who you are and what genuinely matters to you.

Steps To Meeting Your Goals:

1. Taking small steps is the best way to achieve Big Goals.
2. Choose one theme you'd like to set a goal around.
3. Take yourself through a writing process, reflect on your writing, and circle anything that feels like a theme or a pattern.
4. Start small and work up to more challenging or complex goals.

Goal setting and accomplishment are both art and science. When we set off on a path to get from point A to point B, a lot happens on the journey in between. But if you stay the course, you can reach any goal that you set for yourself.

<u>DECLARATION</u>: Today, I set achievable goals for myself and my life. I ask God to help me in this process and on this journey.

Dr. Gail Crowder

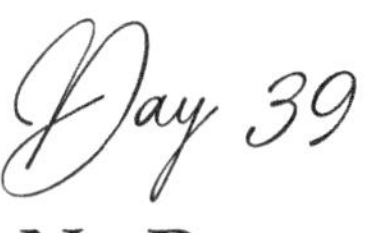

No Regret

DO NOT LOOK back to regret the path of despair. Yesterday is gone, so find ways to rejoice with thanksgiving for the moments of today. Embrace yourself to reflect and dare to dream. Find the truth within your heart, the core of yourself that brings you joy, and anchor it to your mind.

Do not look back to regret the path of despair. Make no excuse for the past; it binds the soul from finding self. Instead, embrace yourself to reflect and dare to dream. Step out of the flow of control onto the path to behold values and beliefs embedded in you that give you peace.

Do not look back to regret the path of despair. Do not let feelings lead your life; trust the values you hold so tight. Instead, embrace yourself to reflect and dare to dream. Embrace life lessons in the here and now without apology for wearing your crown of purpose.

DECLARATION: Today, I will seek God for guidance, putting aside what others say and stepping out in faith to embrace life intentionally with values and beliefs.

Dr. Sharon Foreman

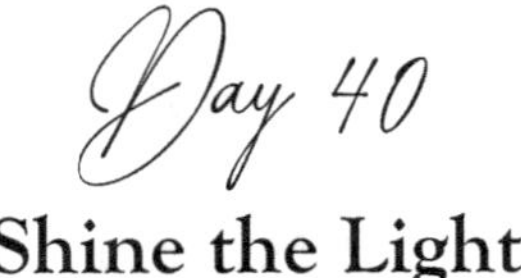

Shine the Light!

GOALS ARE GUIDING lights in your life, illuminating the route ahead and piercing the darkness of fear, distraction, uncertainty, and disappointment. They continually remind you of your value and deepest ambitions, providing you with the fortitude to continue going forward. Each written goal becomes a beacon of hope, illuminating the path to a most gratifying future. They are the light you need in those dark moments, reminding you that you can do great things and that there is a plan for your life.

<u>**DECLARATION**</u>: Today, I will let my goals be the beacon of light to navigate me to achieving my dreams.

Tawawn Lowe

The Ends Justify the Means!

SETTING GOALS CAN be a challenging task for many people. It involves investing time and deep thought and is rarely a straightforward process. In my experience, it is not the act of setting the goal that people struggle with but rather the level of commitment required to achieve it. Dedication is paramount, and it may require sacrificing some of the freedom that one enjoys to manifest the desired outcome. But let me tell you...it's worth it.

Instead of thinking about what it takes to make and accomplish a goal, think about how you will feel when it's done. Think about how your life will be when you check that box off. Think about the results. How much better will your life be by giving your all for this temporary period?

Keep your eyes on the prize. In this instance, the ends will justify the means.

<u>**DECLARATION**</u>: Today, I will keep my eyes on the prize no matter what I see, feel, or do.

Candice Jackson

I Ain't Nothing but A Goal Digger

GOAL-DIGGERS DON'T JUST talk the talk; they walk the walk.

They don't wait for success to come to them; they actively go after it with grit and determination. They embrace the hard work necessary to achieve their ambitions as a vital step on the path to success. Goal-diggers are unrelenting in their pursuit of success and understand that true accomplishment requires putting in the necessary effort. They are not afraid of the efforts, the long hours, or the sacrifices required to get where they want to be. They understand that the journey to success is a marathon, not a sprint, and they are willing to put in the time and energy necessary to see it through.

DECLARATION: Today, I DECLARE; my achievements come from digging and doing the work – I AM A GOAL DIGGER!

Tawawn Lowe

Day 43

Unconscious Goal Setting

DO YOU SET goals to get where you are today? Some may say, "No, I never set goals. I know what I want, and then I go get it." I used to feel this way as well. If I wanted something, I stated that I wanted it, and then "magically, I would achieve it. I now know it wasn't magic, and I also know that regardless of whether I consciously set goals, I took steps to reach my target.

When learning and practicing the art of goal setting, understand that it will feel daunting at first. It is a new language that you don't speak and have never heard but allow yourself to understand and trust the process. Know that you took steps to get there with anything you have achieved. If you were to tell someone how you made it, you could share the steps you took to get there. Those steps were goals. Once you realize you set goals, making this step more conscious becomes easier.

My high school calculus teacher would say, "You know this." You've done this before when we would all get stuck on a problem. It never made any sense to me until this moment. Goal setting is like that, and I'm here to tell you, "You know this. You've done it before."

<u>DECLARATION</u>: Today, I realize I practice goal setting both consciously and unconsciously and will try to bring this practice to the forefront.

Dr. Felicia Pratt

Day 44

Keep the Dream Alive

GOALS WITHOUT ACTION are like a flame without fuel - they flicker and fade away. Writing the vision is just words on a page without the spark of action to bring them to life. They come alive and ignite the fire within you when you take concrete steps toward your goals. Just as faith without work is dead, so are goals without action. It's up to you to fan the flames of your dreams and bring them to life with focused and purposeful action. Don't let your goals die on the pages; bring them to life with your unwavering commitment and effort.

DECLARATION: Today, I will keep my goals alive by taking action that keeps the flame burning in my dreams until I reach my result.

Tawawn Lowe

Day 45

Manifesting the Harvest

MANIFESTING THE FRUIT of your dreams starts with the decisive act of setting goals, but the continuing effort and hard work will produce the harvest. Work towards your goals like a farmer tending to his crop. Tend to the seeds of your goals with care and dedication, nurturing their growth with consistent effort and hard work. Then, commit to the harvesting process and recognize that manifesting the harvest needs daily soil care, watering the seeds, weeding, and getting your hands dirty.

<u>DECLARATION</u>: Today, I affirm that I am the master of my own life and have the power to cultivate and manifest the harvest of my dreams.

Simone Adams

It's Just Me – Celebrating Me!

DON'T WAIT AROUND for people to applaud you; clap for yourself.

The approval of others is not necessary for me to appreciate my successes. I am my biggest cheerleader and will give myself the applause I deserve for every victory.

I understand the power of self-celebration and will embrace it as an essential key part of my journey toward reaching my goals and fulfilling my potential.

Every goal I achieve deserves applause, even some I miss.

<u>**DECLARATION**</u>: Today, I affirm to walk in the power of self-celebration by acknowledging and celebrating my wins, and some missed targets.

Tawawn Lowe

Journey to The End of The Rainbow

GOALS ARE NOT merely intangible aspirations but specific targets that may be attained through effort and commitment. Creating goals requires more than simply stating what you wish to achieve. It is worth the time and effort you invest in planning, strategizing, pursuing, and enduring to achieve your goals.

Everything I/you want, and desire are on the other side of us planning, strategizing, pursuing, and enduring to reach our target.

<u>DECLARATION</u>: Today, I AFFIRM that I can plan and strategize to pursue the rewards that await me on the other side of my goals.

Stephanie Popular

Passing the Torch

WHEN I SET and accomplish my goals, I benefit myself and set an example for the next generation. As a parent, I can inspire and motivate my children to strive for their aspirations. By demonstrating the power of determination, hard work, and goal setting, I am instilling in my children a sense of possibility and a belief in their potential. When I prioritize my goals and achieve them, I show my children that anything is possible with dedication and perseverance. This can be a powerful and transformative lesson for my children, who will grow up to see the world through the lens of possibility and potential rather than limitation and fear.

Ultimately, my success can be a gift to my children, opening doors of opportunity and inspiring them to achieve their dreams.

DECLARATION: Today, I CHOOSE to set goals to demonstrate to my children what they, too, can achieve and become.

Tawawn Lowe

Day 49

"Sometimes We Have to "Hustle!"

HUSTLE IS NOT just a verb; it is the effort it takes to reach your goal and overcome your mistakes. To achieve your goals, you must put in the time and work aggressively to accomplish the objectives in your plan. The hustle may include establishing quality standards, working in the spirit of excellence, completing action items, meeting deadlines, fulfilling commitments, and networking or making connections.

Getting in your flow and moving toward your end results is just the hustle you'll need to reach your goal. It's within your power to hustle, conquer and succeed. Prepare to gird up your strength, energize your spirit, and master your talents. Be ready and willing to hustle and bustle to meet your specific needs.

Make every effort count, and be committed to getting the results you want to achieve.

<u>DECLARATION</u>: Today, I AFFIRM to put more effort into reaching my goal.

Rev. Sandy Williams

Don't Cry Over Spilled Milk

"MISSED GOALS" CAN be seen as a divine intervention to guide you toward your true destiny. While falling short of a goal can be disappointing, it's important to remember that everything happens for a reason. Perhaps what you thought was your goal was not aligned with your true purpose, and missing it is a sign that you are being redirected toward a more fulfilling path. Trust in the universe's wisdom and have faith that everything is working out for your highest good, even if it doesn't always feel that way. Keep moving forward with an open mind and heart, and you will ultimately reach your destined path.

<u>DECLARATION</u>: Today, I CHOOSE to persevere despite any setbacks with an open mind and heart, knowing that I am still on the path that leads me toward fulfilling my true purpose.

Tawawn Lowe

Let Your Goals Bring You Joy

YOU KNOW YOU need goals. You know you need to accomplish certain things. Maybe it's a job, financial independence, a relationship, etc. Whatever it is, don't just make it a job to do or something you have to do. Goals should make you feel passionate. Goals should also bring you joy.

Have fun while you're bringing your goals to life. Stay positive and watch how much more peace you find in this process, even if things don't go as planned. Don't just focus on what you will have but also how you feel. The joy that comes with completion.

<u>DECLARATION</u>: Today, I will focus on the joy I feel when I accomplish my goals.

Candice Jackson

Day 52
Fail Forward

FAILURE IS ONE of the best teachers in life.

Failure to achieve a goal is not a defeat but a valuable opportunity for growth and improvement.

Every time you don't achieve your goals, use it as an opportunity to reflect and learn. Embrace each failure as a chance to learn and adjust your approach and become stronger and more determined in pursuing your goals.

Ask yourself what you can do differently next time and how to use this experience to get closer to becoming and doing better.

Failure is not a permanent state but a stepping stone to success.

Understand that success is not guaranteed and that failures are simply a part of the journey.

Use each experience, both success, and failure, to grow and become better in your pursuit of your goals."

<u>DECLARATION</u>: Today, I CHOOSE to view my failures as opportunities for growth and learning, not failure and defeat.

Tawawn Lowe

"FEAR" To Consider

FOREVER HAVE FAITH in your abilities to accomplish your goals.

Expose yourself to like-minded people who will support and encourage you never to give up, no matter what!

Always focus on the positives when challenging obstacles are met, and...

Remember, persistence wears out resistance, so remain committed to your plan of action until your dream comes true, and then repeat because there's never just one; this is just one of a few.

<u>DECLARATION</u>: Today, I have every right to imagine, proclaim and attain my heart's desires, so go after them, and fear not.

Tia Norde'

My Love Language

TO ME, GOAL setting is a declaration of love for myself. I express my love for myself every time I set goals. It's a tender expression of my commitment to becoming my best self, realizing my full potential, and living a life of purpose. Through setting goals, doing the work to achieve them, and charting my progress, I am nurturing my growth and fostering a deep and abiding love for the person I am and the person I strive to be, the life I want, and the legacy I want to leave. Whether big or small, each goal I set is a reminder that I am worthy of my dreams and have the power to shape my destiny.

<u>DECLARATION</u>: Today, I AFFIRM my love for myself by setting meaningful goals and taking inspired action towards their realization.

Tawawn Lowe

Small Goals, Quick Wins

IF THIS IS the first time you've made goals, or you have made goals you have not yet accomplished, I suggest you make them smaller. Not in the sense that the goal is small. But instead, you break down big goals into smaller ones. Smaller multiple goals that you can accomplish in a shorter time frame. You need to see quick wins. Quick wins help you stay consistent and focused. They build your momentum because you see the value in your work to accomplish your goal.

Start with your main goal. Then break down everything that must happen for the goal to become a reality. That breaks all those things down to everyday tasks. Now you can celebrate your accomplishments every day. Before you know it, your main goal is complete.

Let's get these quick wins!

<u>DECLARATION</u>: Today, I CHOOSE to take one small step toward my goal and celebrate the WIN!

Candice Jackson

Beyond the Pot of Gold

GOALS ARE LIKE rainbows, offering a sense of wonder, possibility, and promise. However, they require effort and patience, overcoming obstacles, taking risks, and staying committed to the end result. While the prize may seem distant or impossible at times, the journey toward it can be filled with beauty, growth, and discovery. By staying committed to your goals, you can enjoy the process of reaching for the rainbow and ultimately bask in the light of your achievements.

<u>DECLARATION</u>: Today, I AFFIRM that my goals are like rainbows, leading me toward manifesting all my dreams.

Tawawn Lowe

Day 57

It is Done!

CROSSING THE FINISH line of a race is an exhilarating feeling, just like accomplishing a long-held life goal. First, however, we must begin our initial preparation with the final accomplishment at the forefront of our minds. We must also answer some very vital questions. How do I reach my goal?

What plan of action must I put in place? What major and minor milestones will it take? And we must address this important dilemma, what contingencies and alternatives do I have if obstacles get in my way? Obtaining goals is no easy feat. It takes planning and execution. It takes patience and tenacity when initial plans fall apart. Having a mentor and a network of supporters is another key element to helping us reach our goals. Then, when we cross that distant finish line and finally accomplish our goal, we can say hooray and thank you. Hooray, I made it. Thank you, Lord, for guiding me, and thank you to those who supported me along the way. It is done!

<u>**DECLARATION**</u>: Today, I AFFIRM, "It is done!"

Rev. Sandy Williams

The Power of Writing Your Goals

THERE IS SOMETHING magical about putting your goals down on paper. It's like casting a spell that brings your dreams to life. Writing your goals is not just a simple exercise; it's a transformative process. It gives you clarity, focus, and purpose. It allows you to turn your abstract desires into concrete and achievable objectives. When you write your goals, you bring them into existence, and the universe conspires to make them happen.

So don't wait; start writing your goals today. Make the magic happen.

Let your written goals guide you toward a purpose, joy, and successful life. Trust the process, and trust in the power of the written word. Your future self will thank you."

<u>DECLARATION</u>: Today, I AFFIRM the power of the written word and the magic of manifestation.

Tawawn Lowe

Potential in Waiting!

GOALS ARE LIKE potential in waiting; all you must do is achieve them. With each achievement, you unlock levels of accomplishment, boosting your confidence and catapulting you towards a heightened level of self.

This benefits your overall well-being in self-appreciation, love, and acceptance. When you are successful in your accomplishments, admiration builds, and opportunities grow. So, start achieving smaller goals now, in preparation and practice towards achieving bigger ones. It is better to start small than not at all.

You don't have to win big for it to count; the small wins are wins too! It's not about how you start; it's how you finish and follow through. So, pace yourself, and remain persistent and steady.

The next opportunity may be THE ONE, so stay ready!

Potential waiting or potential in waiting? Persistent, steady, and ready on your mark to set your GOALS.

<u>DECLARATION</u>: Today, I AFFIRM to be persistent ready, set, and to go for my goals.

Tia Norde'

Day 60
G.O.A.L.S.

G – God Guiding You Towards Greatness

O – Operating in Obedience, Open to new Opportunities, Overcoming Obstacles, Objectives with Outstanding Outcomes

A – Awareness of self, Achieving Aspirations, with an Abundance Attitude and mindset

L – Leveraging LIFE with Love, Learning, Lessons, and self-Leadership to create a Legacy

S – Spirituality, Self-love, Self-care, and Self-worth interconnect as a Synergetic force.

<u>DECLARATION</u>: Today, I embrace G.O.A.L.S. - guiding principles that lead me toward personal growth and development.

Tawawn Lowe

INTENTIONAL LIVING

Taking responsibility for your life and owning your power to create the kind of life you desire. It's about embracing your unique gifts and talents and using them to impact your life and the world around you positively. It's about living with purpose, passion, and intentionality and creating a life that reflects who you are and what you value.

Beloved,

You didn't just happen. The Lord chose you. He had you in mind when he made you. God has a purpose and a plan for your life, and He wants you to go after it with all your heart.

You've been given the chance for a happy and prosperous life. You were born for a reason, and one of your primary goals is to deliberate in your living. You were not created to wander through life without a direction or purpose, waiting for life to happen, but to make life happen for you. You were born to live your life by design.

Living life by design is an intentional process where you craft a life that gives you meaning and satisfaction because you've taken the time to be, deliberate and plan it out. It paves the way for a life filled with meaning and purpose by encouraging you to get to know yourself on a deep, personal level, to respect, value, and appreciate yourself for who you are and what you bring to the world, to love yourself without condition, and to put yourself first in all aspects of your life.

This intentional approach requires you to take ownership of your life and actively pursue a path toward success and fulfillment. It means proactively shaping your future and making choices that align with your values and aspirations. It also involves prioritizing personal growth and development and being open to new experiences and opportunities to help you achieve your goals.

Living a life by design is all about intentionality. Intentionality requires you to focus on your being, becoming, personal growth, and success in every aspect of your life. It demands courage, determination, and a willingness to take risks and step outside your comfort zone. It involves challenging yourself, embracing new experiences, and continuously learning and growing.

Now you must decide how you will live your life. Will it be intentional and by design, or will it occur by default?

  EVERYBODY NEEDS A LITTLE TLC

Day 61

I AM Intentional....

I AM intentional with my being and becoming,
I AM intentional with my finances and wealth,
I AM intentional with my goals,
I AM intentional with my health,
I AM intentional about my mindset,
I AM intentional with my peace,
I AM intentional about my personal development,
I AM intentional about my professional success,
I AM intentional about my purpose,
I AM intentional with my self-love (forever loving me unconditionally),
I AM intentional with my self-care,
I AM intentional about my spiritual growth,
I AM intentional about my success,
I AM intentional with my relationships,
I AM intentional with my time,
I AM intentional with my thoughts, and
I AM intentional with my words.

<u>DECLARATION</u>: Today, I focus on the aspects crucial to my personal and professional well-being.

Tawawn Lowe

Day 62

Live Life on Purpose.

MAKING SOUND DECISIONS about what you say and do is intentional living. To cleanse your mind of negative thoughts is something you do on purpose. To seek knowledge and continue to be a lifetime learner is how you intentionally cultivate your mind. To think good thoughts toward others is a process of shaping a heart of love. Deciding to live a lifestyle of good eating habits and exercise to maintain a healthy body shows you care about yourself. To read the word of God demonstrates your desire to grow spiritually. To do what has been placed in your heart and show up to live your desired life is intentional living. It's within you to "Live Life on Purpose."

<u>**DECLARATION:**</u> Today, I CHOOSE to begin and continue to live out my good intentions.

Rev. Sandy Williams

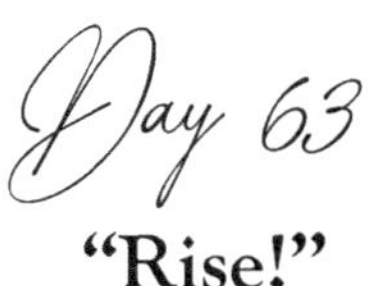

"Rise!"

STAY ON CRUISE control when hot-head communications run amuck. Just because they're flying off the handle doesn't mean you must.

Silence can be golden, listen and observe. It doesn't pay to wrestle with a donkey, or any beast, for that matter, physically or with words.

You're above all that; stop stooping to their level; they're trying to pull you down, to knock you off your game, like crabs in a barrel.

The analogy is real, don't get fooled by the disguise; your social circle needs to mature with you or fall by the waste side.

Set your boundaries, stand your ground, determine what type of party this is, and how you wanna get down.

People will take advantage of every chance they get, no matter the cost or whom they offend, as long as it works out for them in the end.

Relationships with people can be fickle; they leave you in a pickle when you're in a bind. Their word isn't their bond, their two cents aren't worth a penny, their honesty isn't worth Sugar-Honey-Iced-Tea, and when they need money, they come to you, but if you need, they never have any.

Birds of a feather do flock together, so don't be a do-do bird or a chicken, soar with eagles above the clouds, make rising above your mission!

<u>DECLARATION</u>: Today, I CHOOSE not to settle and remain at a ground-level vantage point that doesn't work for me anymore; today, I will strive towards my maximum potential, and like an eagle, I shall soar!

Tia Norde'

Flip the Switch

EVER NOTICE HOW easy it is to name the things you don't want in life?

Debt, drama, disease, Danger?

But when asked, "What do you want?" You are hesitant to get precise.

Flip the Switch

Become well acquainted with that which brings you joy.

The next time you find yourself focused on the "I don't want" narrative. STOP and ask yourself what it is that you want.

If something doesn't work, switch the internal conversation to "what will work." Answer - how will you know when 'that' something is working?

Ensure you do not spend most of your time dodging and swerving from what you don't want.

Switch out of that mode and move forward to what you want. Get familiar with what that YES looks like and how it makes you feel.

Let your narrative be strong and affirming.

<u>DECLARATION</u>: Today, I CHOOSE to speak in affirmation of the things that I want and desire. I am giving energy and Breathing intention to the elements that nourish me.

Tia Hall

Day 65

Your Presence = Present!

MAKE IT A habit of only engaging in safe and healthy relationships. Your engagements should be more of a safe haven and less of a battlefield. Guard yourself against harmful and toxic relations. Be intentional about the people you associate with and spend time with. This world has enough toxicity, so you don't need to add or engage in it. Pushing past your faults and avoiding negativity will free you from self-doubt. Things are clearing up for you; set your mind for peace. Shift your mindset to only positive thoughts. Better yet, wake up and have conversations that are intentionally non-judgmental.

You can make your presence known by showing up with a positive attitude. There's no time to be afraid of yourself. Whether it is a new opportunity or challenge that arrives on your doorstep, instead of focusing on the issues or problems, try focusing on the steps that will lead you to success. If we always do what's right, the rest will come.

No doubt about it, when you walk in your purpose boldly, your presence will be made known. Never forget the difference you've made. You can draw from the past and lead to the future. Your contributions do matter. Although it may be tempting, don't allow yourself to compare yourself with others. You gotta be you – I gotta be me.

Yes, I'm present, and being present means, I must be a gift! So, I'll be the gift that keeps on giving!

<u>**DECLARATION**</u>: Today, I CHOOSE to be present and walk in my purpose.

Yolanda "Loni" Chinn

Tune out the Noise!

THERE ARE SO many distractions in the world. You may wake up with a plan, be focused, and BAM, life happens. You change one direction, and then you change another. Before you know it, everything you intended for the day doesn't get done.

To truly live an intentional life, you must stay focused. Roll with the changes, but always bring yourself right back. Allow for some deviation but not a change in direction. Don't allow what other people want, what society says, or what social media shows you to distract you from your plans.

Let all of this be the noise you tune so you can manifest.

DECLARATION: Today, I CHOOSE to stay focused, quickly adjust to distractions, and maintain my direction.

Candice Jackson

Day 67

Living Your Life Like It's Golden

AN INTENTIONAL LIFE creates more thought than an unintentional life. You must make conscious decisions and question your thoughts and actions. Seek to be more aware of your desires and choose your behaviors accordingly. Habits can be the bane of intentional living unless you choose your habits intentionally.

Steps to living an intentional life:

1. **Evaluate your behavior.** To live an intentional life, you must evaluate and understand yourself. Why do you do the things you do? Why do you fail to do the things you don't do?

2. **What motivates your actions each day?** Are you moving toward short-term pleasure or avoiding short-term pain? Or are your actions directed toward an intended purpose?

3. **Know your values and beliefs.** Knowing your values and beliefs can make it easier to live intentionally.

4. **Know your intentions for each day.** For example, your intention for today might be to avoid any spending that isn't necessary. On the other hand, a long-term intention might be to be debt-free.

5. **Choose your habits.** Most of your habits seemed to develop on their own. It's important to choose your habits. Habits can mask your intentions by removing the thought process from the equation.

<u>DECLARATION</u>: Today, I CHOOSE to be mindful of my intentions, thoughts, actions, and goals.

Dr. Gail Crowder

Recipe for Intentional Living

1 cup of self-belief

1 cup of discipline

1 cup of self-love

2-3 dashes of intentional action

1 cup of courage

1 cup of focus

1 cup of commitment

1 Stirring Spoon

Instructions:

Preheat your mindset to be open and positive. Gather all the ingredients, and begin stirring in the ingredients, one at a time, starting with self-belief to infuse your heart and mind with confidence. Next, add courage, discipline, focus, and commitment to help you overcome your fears, and life distractions, stay on track, keep your eyes on the prize, and never give up. Stir in self-love to remind you to love yourself unconditionally, flaws and all. Finally, add the dashes of intentional action, stir thoroughly until all ingredients are fully blended, and form into success habits. Use the success habits with your dreams, goals, and purpose to create beautiful dishes of personal and professional success.

<u>DECLARATION</u>: Today, I CHOOSE to use success ingredients to be and live an intentional life.

Tawawn Lowe

Day 69

Tapestry of life

CHOOSE THE PATH designed with grace uniquely designed for you to embrace – the tapestry of life. Lay down the passive things of dormant dreams and stolen goals. Redeem the values of the heart to unite your vision in the light intentionally.

The visions dimmed are no more, lost talents behind locked doors freed again to embrace the tapestry of life. Behold the possibilities of life; let them reign day and night on canvas, weaved with self-held goals set free by faith. Redeem the values of the heart to unite your vision in the light intentionally.

The life you live is up to you, so try to understand the rules. If you choose a life without grace, you lose the strength to embrace the tapestry of life meant for you. So, choose the One who filled your head with dreams and goals for life's canvas. Redeem the values of the heart to unite your vision in the light intentionally.

<u>**DECLARATION:**</u> Today, I CHOOSE to seek the giver of grace, putting aside what others say, to run the race following my values and beliefs to shape the tapestry of life intentionally.

Dr. Sharon Foreman

What are You doing it For?

WHEN TRYING TO achieve something big, we are always asked what is your why? Your why is the thing that will keep you going when times are difficult. Your why is supposed to drive you and keep you going, which is very important. Without a bigger meaning, it may be easy to throw in the towel. But there is another question I want to challenge you to ask yourself, and that is what I am doing this for; what is the purpose?

When you begin to outline your goals and the activities that will help you achieve those goals, ask yourself what the purpose of this activity is. This will allow you to know why you are doing a specific activity and particular to ensure you live intentionally. Some actions may not be related to your goal, but you can still ask yourself, what is the purpose of this activity? An example would be staying at a job to be considered vested in the organization to receive the benefits one may receive. Another example could be health-related. For example, you may go to the gym because not only does it help you reach your weight loss goals, it makes you feel good or it helps to clear your mind.

Living intentionally starts with asking yourself what the purpose of this specific activity is. Then, you are conscious of the activities you are doing and the goals you plan to achieve.

<u>**DECLARATION:**</u> Today, I will ask myself what the purpose of this activity is so that I can practice intentional living.

Dr. Felicia Pratt

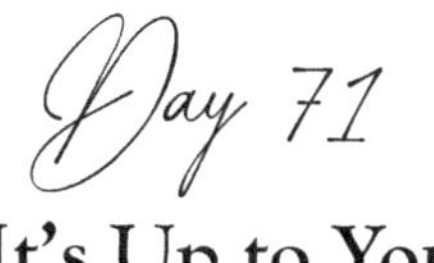

It's Up to You

YOU ARE THE CEO of you, so boss up; you are in charge of you.

As the CEO of you, it is up to you to make choices that will help you live intentionally in every way. Instead of letting your life slip by without a plan, you must decide to take control of it and steer it in the direction you desire. Then, you get to choose the action you will take to get you closer to becoming the person you want to be and the kind of life you want for yourself.

<u>**DECLARATION**</u>: Today, I CHOOSE to make the conscious decision to be purposeful about the course my life takes and the person I evolve into.

Tawawn Lowe

Believe in Yourself and Make it Happen!

AN INTENTIONAL LIFESTYLE is giving yourself your deepest desires and shining light upon the world. They work together for your benefit when you put your mind and energy behind anything. This way of living emphasizes both ambitious aspirations and practical, attainable targets. With a clear purpose in mind, you enjoy each moment to the fullest, knowing you are worthy of the finest that life has to offer. You can make anything happen because of your optimistic outlook and self-assurance.

DECLARATION: Today, I DECLARE; I am confident in my abilities and trust that I have what it takes to make it happen.

Stephanie Popular

Self-Talk with Love

THE POWER OF your self-talk cannot be underestimated. Your words have the power to shape your thoughts, emotions, actions, and, ultimately, your reality. That's why it is essential to be intentional and purposeful with the words you choose to speak to yourself.

Life and death are in the power of your tongue, so it is crucial to be accountable for the words you speak. Be conscious of the words you choose to say to yourself, and make sure they are empowering, uplifting, and life-giving.

Your self-talk should align with your values, goals, and aspirations and bring value to your life. Choose words that inspire confidence, courage, and resilience, and let them fuel you toward achieving your dreams. By being intentional with your self-talk, you can transform your mindset and unleash your full potential.

Remember, the words you speak have the power to shape your life, so choose them wisely.

<u>DECLARATION</u>: Today, I CHOOSE to engage in life-affirming, positive self-talk today, being careful of the words I speak to myself, and replacing negative thoughts with those that speak of life, light, and love.

Tawawn Lowe

Day 74

Follow Through

PURPOSE IN YOUR heart to focus and follow through to complete all you envision and desire to achieve. Stop procrastinating and overcome that which you imagine as a limitation. You may have to let go of bad habits or unproductive practices to live a life that follows through on your good intentions. You may have to put forth extra effort; you may have to pause and rethink, restructure, or reroute your course of action. If you encounter detours, they will redirect you and not abort your plan. Changing your course of action may lead to a better outcome. Press, push, and produce! Don't let life discourage you, overwhelm you, or stop you. Stand firm in what you want to accomplish or achieve. What has been instilled in you is meant to manifest.

<u>**DECLARATION**</u>: Today, I CHOOSE to focus and work on what's next.

Rev. Sandy Williams

Day 75

"Last Chance"

<u>ATTENTION READER</u>: THIS is your last chance to rescue your future from the stagnant demise it's heading toward because you refuse to take a step out on faith to believe in yourself. How many great ideas must enter your mind before you grab hold of one and become whom you've always imagined you could be? It's not just a crazy idea or some off-the-wall thought; it's your inner CEO, Entrepreneur self, trying to tell you something.

Whatsoever ye thinketh shall be, so what do you think of yourself and your capabilities? Based on your present circumstances, I'm sure you feel capable of more, so why not act on it and expound on new possibilities? Life is about living, not just existing, and you only get one life, so recognize and maximize the opportunities right in front of you! You are the artist, so create a masterpiece of beauty that will have people in reverie over your accomplishments, aspiring to achieve a quality of life for themselves that would have been overlooked had it not been for your example and testimony.

<u>DECLARATION</u>: Today, I CHOOSE not to let another day go by thinking of the past and what could have been while dismissing the present, what could be, and the future, what's yet to come. There's still time; I can't waste it!

Tia Norde'

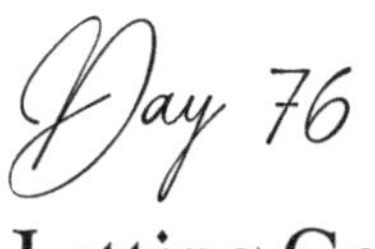

Day 76
Letting Go

PERPETUAL LIVING IN mourning will keep you from what God has new for you. The quicker you let go of all hurts will, be easier to heal. Allow the healing to begin by becoming an expert in letting things go. You must forgive. Forgiveness should be a continual daily action. Let it go.

Develop a continuous forgiving heart so that you can forgive daily. Let it go. God will give you beauty for those ashes. Live in a state of perpetual forgiveness. When you do this, disappointments won't stop you. Instead, you'll experience joy, happiness, and freedom when you release it.

DECLARATION: Today, I CHOOSE to let it go! I will learn to continue to forgive myself and others.

Yolanda "Loni" Chinn

Improve your Mental Health

DID YOU KNOW that living an intentional life can help improve your mental health? Studies have shown many benefits to being intentional. My therapist has said the same, and I have seen the benefits in my life. Being clear on what you want and who you are brings so much clarity. Here are a few benefits you can look forward to by living intentionally:

- Easy decision-making – you don't have to go back and forth about what you should do. You already know if it fits your core values.
- Peace – you focus on what you can control, not what you can't.
- Healthy relationships – your focus helps create healthy boundaries, which results in healthy relationships.

I could go on and on with the list. But do you see where I am going? Maybe the one thing you need to have more positivity in your life is to live intentionally toward your beliefs and values.

<u>**DECLARATION:**</u> Today, I CHOOSE to be committed and intentional about my mental health.

Candice Jackson

Day 78

Intentional with my Financial Self-Care

BE DELIBERATE AND mindful of your actions for your financial well-being.

As you prioritize self-care, such as physical and emotional health, paying attention to your financial health is equally important. Being intentional with your financial self-care means regularly checking in with your money mindset and habits, identifying areas for growth and improvement, and taking concrete steps towards achieving your financial goals.

By making intentional choices and actions, you can cultivate a healthy and abundant relationship with money and, ultimately, thrive in your financial life.

<u>DECLARATION</u>: Today, I AFFIRM to engage in financial self-care. I will be intentional with my money and make choices that align with my financial goals and values.

Tawawn Lowe

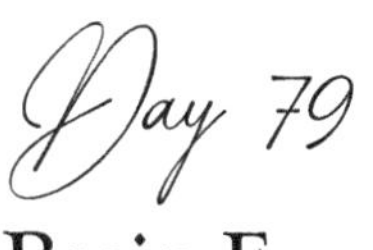

Brain Food

WHAT DO YOU feed your mind? You must be intentional about what you feed your mind.

Be careful and make sure you are exposing yourself to mainly positive energy. Your thoughts can direct your actions, so do pay attention to what you take in. Nourishing your mind is essential to your self-care. Feed your brain with knowledge and learn something new daily. Affirm you with affirmations, meditation, prayer, inspirational writings, and music. You've probably heard, "The mind is a terrible thing to waste," So I challenge you to use it wisely. What you feed your mind can ultimately feed your soul, and it sets the path of your attitude and mindset.

<u>DECLARATION</u>: Today, I will be intentional about what I feed my mind. I will provide it with only pure intentions.

Yolanda "Loni" Chinn

Ka-Ching – My Money Matters!

I GOT MY money on my mind, which keeps me dedicated and determined to achieve financial freedom.

To harness money's power, you must practice money mindfulness. Be deliberate and focus on every aspect of your financial life, from your mindset to your habits. Aligning these elements with your goals and values can transform money from a source of stress and uncertainty to a tool that works for you. With intentionality and a mindful approach, you can unlock your finances' full potential and achieve the desired financial freedom you want.

<u>DECLARATION</u>: Today, I CHOOSE to focus on my financial aspirations and take intentional actions toward turning my financial dreams into a reality.

Tawawn Lowe

Day 81

Do the Right Thing

TAKING THE TIME to consider whether a wrong way is right or whether the right way is wrong is contemplation. We must examine our decisions and actions thoughtfully and fairly, not only for ourselves but for others. Doing the right thing can be easy, and it can also be hard, especially if the right way is not what we have been taught. Unlearning negative behavior or negative thinking is a challenge and difficult to overcome.

But doing the right thing has its own set of rewards and satisfaction.

Do the right thing and see the smile of approval that beams your way. Do the right thing and stand tall as you get the pat on your back. Know that a smile and a pat on your back are not the incentives for doing the right thing. Do the right thing and know that you only need the approval of what's within your heart. Do the right thing and show the world the love and joy you have reflected in doing the right thing. You may lose a friend and defeat a foe, but doing the right thing will bring you great satisfaction and peace.

Be intentional and do the right thing.

<u>**DECLARATION**</u>: Today, I CHOOSE my intentions to do the right thing.

Rev. Sandy Williams

Change Starts with You

WHEN YOU GET to the point, you can't take it anymore- you'll do something about it.

When you're tired of being sick and tired, you'll do something about it.

When enough is enough, you'll be ready to take the leap and make the necessary changes. Success takes a tremendous amount of action. Not all at one time, but actionable movement is required. It will require you to become disciplined with your grind, operating out of normalcy. I dare you to do something different.

<u>**DECLARATION**</u>: Today, I CHOOSE to start with becoming the change I want.

Yolanda "Loni" Chinn

Day 83

On Purpose

WHAT DO YOU look forward to each day that makes you get out of bed and get going? Is there anything? If not, then, "Houston, we have a problem!" Each day there should be something that motivates you to get up and get going, so find out what you love that will do that for you. It doesn't have to be a person; it can be a place or a thing, just something that will drive you to do something other than remain stagnant. Life is meant to be lived, in motion, with vibrance and intention, so begin to live your life on purpose, doing everything on purpose, with purpose! Smile at yourself and random people on purpose because it's fun and feels good; be kind to yourself and others because you can and should; do a good deed for yourself and another on purpose to brighten your and someone else's day. These are just a few ideas to start with to get the ball rolling! The more you become intentional about living your life, the happier you'll be.

<u>**DECLARATION**</u>**:** Today, I CHOOSE to live life, in motion, with vibrance and intention, on purpose, with purpose!

Tia Norde'

Living Each Day with Intentions

INTENTIONAL DAYS ARE the building blocks of a purposeful life. When you approach each day with intention and purpose, you can focus your energy on the things that matter most to you.

Living with intention means owning your life and recognizing that you can create the life you want. It means being proactive rather than reactive and taking deliberate action to achieve your goals. This can involve setting clear intentions, creating daily routines that support your goals, and regularly checking in with yourselves to ensure you are on track.

By living intentionally, you can create your life on purpose - one that is fulfilling, meaningful, and aligned with your values. This means living a life that is true to yourselves rather than simply going through the motions. It means creating a vision for your life and working towards it with purpose and determination.

<u>DECLARATION</u>: Today, I AFFIRM to live each day with intention, approach each moment mindfully, with a clear purpose and a sense of direction, to create a life that is meaningful, fulfilling, and authentic to who I am.

Tawawn Lowe

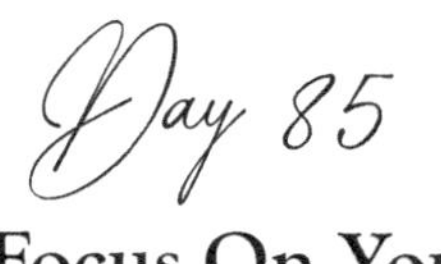

Focus On You

BE TRUE TO who you are. Don't let anyone take that away from you. Nobody in the world can do you- the way you do. So don't be afraid to be honest, to dare to be different.

Focus on you every day. Organize your day to include what you need to do for yourself and concentrate on what you need to be successful. Being truthful about who you are while pursuing what you want may not come easy, but it's worth it. After all, aren't you worth it?

So, give that pursuit everything you've got.

DECLARATION: Today, I CHOOSE, focus on my needs, and emphasize that I am important too.

Yolanda "Loni" Chinn

Day 86

Practical Everyday Intention

"LIVING AN INTENTIONAL life" sounds like a buzz phrase. A phrase that makes you excited until you go home and realize you don't know how to do it. It seems like such a big thing to tackle. I'm here to tell you that you probably already live intentionally but don't know it. Knowing you already do it in everyday tasks can motivate you to keep going. It will show you that you can do it. Here is how you can live intentionally every day:

- Create and stick to a budget – you intend for your money to pay for this and buy that,
- Be active – you intend to live a healthy life, so you do something active,
- Grocery shopping – you intend to eat this meal for dinner,
- Record your favorite show – you intend to unwind after work, so you record your favorite show to watch later.

See? You're already living an intentional life. Think about what else you do. Put an "I intend" next to the why you do it. Now repeat that process for every other action you take.

DECLARATION: Today, I INTEND to "_____________" (fill in the blank with a different activity every day). Examples: "Today, I intend to go for a 30 min walk after dinner". I intend to take my lunch break away from my desk".

Candice Jackson

Present Moment Breathing

BE INTENTIONAL WITH your breathing, stop waiting to exhale, and let every breath you take count.

Stop holding your breath; let your breath be a divine exchange that allows you to release.

Your breath is a powerful tool that you can use to cultivate a sense of calm and clarity in your lives. With every inhale, you can imagine taking in positive energy, envisioning it flowing into every cell of your body and filling you with a sense of vitality and renewal. As you exhale, you can release any negative thoughts or emotions that no longer serve you, letting go of stress, tension, and anxiety.

Being intentional with your breathing allows it to connect with your inner self, enabling you to gain clarity and insight into your thoughts and feelings. Just breathe because it helps you stay centered and present, to be more aware of your surroundings, and be fully engaged in the present moment. Be intentional with each inhale and exhale to cultivate and create a sense of balance, harmony, peace, and relaxation within yourselves.

So, take a deep breath, inhale positivity, and exhale negativity. Let your breath be a source of renewal and empowerment, allowing you to live with intention and purpose.

<u>DECLARATION</u>: Today, I AFFIRM to be intentional with my breath, focusing on each inhale and exhale, connecting with the present moment, bringing peace and clarity, and releasing negative thoughts or emotions.

Tawawn Lowe

Put a Smile on It!

WHEN LIFE SEEMS grim and you feel out of place, putting a smile on your face is always beneficial.

When tears well up in your eyes, and you want to cry your fears away, that's the very moment to call on your faith and put a smile on your face. Not to deny your feelings or drown out your doubt but to uplift your spirit and see life in a brand-new light. A smile to frame your face, a smile to shine for others to see, a smile with the intention to bring peace, warmth, and harmony.

When you stand in the presence of ridicule and rejection, offer a smile to ward off disappointment and depression. When hardships knock you down and the path you walk is rough. Get up, brush off the disgust, and bring forth a smile to help clear the way for a better day. Smile with the intent to bless those who pass your way and smile with the unction to overcome thoughts that will make you sad and blue. Put a smile on your face to show love and affection. There's nothing better than a big bubbling smile when spoken words will not do. Let your smile be the joy of life that comes shining through.

Smile from your heart to show kindness and that you care. Be the smile others need to see, and continue to smile happily.

<u>DECLARATION</u>: Today, I CHOOSE to put a smile on my face.

Rev. Sandy Williams

Make Your Existence Matter

IF YOU'RE READING this, you're not DEAD.

Every day you wake up is another opportunity for you to rise up! Rise and Shine! You can continue to move; although you may be weary, tired, and feeling defeated, you have yet another chance to get it going. Now is your time. It's time for you to stop chasing misery and start chasing your dreams. Become a doer and electrify the energy, perhaps rejuvenate the energy you once had. Do what will take you higher? Ask yourself, will complaining help you to be the best of who you are?

I dare you to change your mindset. Especially if what you're currently doing isn't working for you. Lack of effort is a dream killer. You must do something; do the work it takes to be successful. Find out what you need to do – then do it. Become a continuous learner, an obedient student striving for success. You were not born just to exist.

Believe you can do it! Know that you can! Make your existence matter!

<u>**DECLARATION**</u>: Today, I CHOOSE not to procrastinate. I will make my existence matter.

Yolanda "Loni" Chinn

Every Moment Counts

TIME IS A precious and finite resource; we are all given the same 24 hours daily. How we choose to use those hours can significantly impact the quality of our lives. When we are intentional with our time, we are purposeful in our actions and make conscious decisions that align with our values and goals.

Use your time wisely, prioritize what matters most, and be mindful of how you spend each moment. Set boundaries and say no to activities or people that drain your energy or do not serve your greater purpose. It means being fully present now, whether in the moment, working on a project, spending time with loved ones, or simply taking a few minutes to reflect and recharge. When you are not intentional with your time, you risk getting caught up in distractions and wasting precious moments you can never return.

So, recognize the value of your time and use it wisely.

<u>DECLARATION</u>: Today, I CHOOSE to use my time wisely, prioritize the things that matter most because every moment counts, and I choose to make the most of every moment.

Tawawn Lowe

About the Visionary of Everybody Needs A Little TLC

TAWAWN LOWE IS the proud mother of two beautiful daughters, a GlamMa, a loving daughter, a good friend, and associate to many, a #1 Amazon bestselling author, philanthropist, serial entrepreneur, transformational life-strategist coach, and mentor. She is the CEO of TLConsultancy, LLC, the Founder of the Women Walking in Their Own Shoes Movement and Foundation, and the sole proprietor of Tea Lovers Cafe and TLC-Publishing Company.

Tawawn uses her multidimensional consulting and coaching practice to help her clients be intentional about their being, connecting their life or business visions with goals to achieve success through accountability, facilitation, inspiration, coaching, and other dynamic mechanisms. She has combined her life experiences of navigating limited self-belief and fear of success, 25+ years of professional experiences, and multiple certifications (Life Coach, MBTI Certified Practitioner, Prosci ADKAR Change Management, and Facilitation to bring forth change, transformation to individuals, and organizations.

Tawawn is inherently committed to emboldening women, specifically women 40+, desperately seeking greater fulfillment and purpose for the next chapter of their life.

She has created the Everybody Needs A Little TLC Trilogy to support individuals' investment into their personal development and their journey of becoming their best selves and creating their best lives. These books are also excellent tools for leaders, organizations, non-profits, and social services programs that support clients' personal development, therapists, social workers, trainers, and book clubs. These books can be offered at wholesale prices.

For additional information on TLConsultancy, please visit Tawawn at:
www.tawawn.com

You can connect with Tawawn here:
Email: TL@tawawnlowe.com
Facebook: https://www.facebook.com/TawawnLConsultancy
Instagram: https://www.instagram.com/tl_consultancy/

EVERYBODY NEEDS A LITTLE TLC – TRILOGY

Series 1

Series 2

Order Today www.tlcbookseries.com

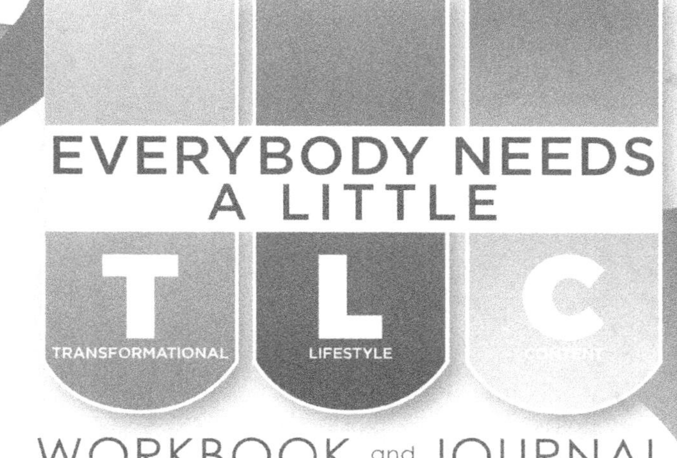

WORKBOOK and JOURNAL

A Journey to Self-Discovery, Prioritizing You, and Intentional Living

PRESENTED BY

TAWAWN LOWE